CUB'S BIG WORLD

Sarah L. Thomson

Illustrated by Joe Cepeda

HARCOURT CHILDREN'S BOOKS
Houghton Mifflin Harcourt
Boston   New York   2013

Cub knew all about the world.

It was smooth

and white

and cool.

Inside the world

were Mom

and Cub.

And that was all.

Mom was big

and white

and warm.

Her nose was black.

Her fur was soft.

Her milk was sweet.

Cub could hear her heart

beat *thump, thump, thump.*

Cub's world was good.

One day Mom poked
her black nose
through the wall of the world.
Cub scrambled outside
after her.

The light was bright.

It made Cub blink.

The wind was strong.

It ruffled Cub's fur.

The sky was a color

Cub had never seen.

"Blue," said Mom.

"Blue," whispered Cub.

Cub found a hill.

Step by step by step,

she went up and up and up.

At the top she stopped

and stared.

The world was big,

BIG,

BIG!

Oops!

The world was slippery, too.

Down, down, down.

Fast, fast, fast!

The world was fun!

Cub slid to a stop.

She looked around.

White hills.

White valleys.

White to the edge
of the bright, bright blue.

But where was Mom?

Cub sat and thought.
Mom's nose was black.
Cub looked for one black thing
in a white, white world.

There was Mom!
Cub ran.

Squawk!

A raven flapped away.

There was Mom!
Cub leaped.

Swish!
An ermine flicked its tail.

There was Mom!
Cub pounced.

Splash!

A seal dived way down deep.

The world was too big

for a cub with no mom.

Cub was brave.

She found another hill.

Step by step by step,

she went up

and up

and up.

From here, she thought,

I will see Mom.

But all she saw was snow.

Snow in her eyes.

Snow in her ears.

Snow in her face

as she tumbled

and rolled

between two big paws

and was kissed

by one black nose.

"Dear Cub," said Mom.
"The world is big.
I'll be close by
till you're big, too."

Mom's fur was soft.

Her voice was sweet.

Her heart beat

thump, thump, thump.

"Home," whispered Cub.

Cub's world was good.

For my cub—s.l.t.

For Beauty, who made it home—j.c.

Text copyright © 2013 by Sarah L. Thomson
Illustrations copyright © 2013 by Cepeda Studio Inc.

Harcourt Children's Books is an imprint of Houghton Mifflin Harcourt Publishing Company.

www.hmhbooks.com

The illustrations in this book were done in oil and acrylic on illustration board.
The text was set in Bryant.
The display type was set in Populaire.

Library of Congress Cataloging-in-Publication Data
Thomson, Sarah L.
Cub's big world / Sarah L. Thomson ; illustrated by Joe Cepeda.
pages cm
Summary: "In this picture book about exploring the big snowy world,
a tiny polar bear learns that she can be brave—
especially with Mom close by."—Provided by publisher.
ISBN 978-0-544-05739-5
[1. Polar bear—Fiction. 2. Bears—Fiction. 3. Animals—Infancy—Fiction. 4. Mother and child—Fiction.]
I. Cepeda, Joe, illustrator. II. Title.
PZ7.T378Cu 2013
[E]—dc23
2012045056

Manufactured in China
SCP 10 9 8 7 6 5 4 3 2 1
4500427165